QUARTERBACKS!

EIGHTEEN OF FOOTBALL'S GREATEST

George Sullivan

Atheneum Books for Young Readers

ALL "FOOTBALL CARD" PHOTOS ARE USED COURTESY OF WIDE WORLD
EXCEPT FOR PAGES 30 AND 33, COURTESY OF GEORGE SULLIVAN, AND
PAGE 57, COURTESY OF THE NEW YORK PUBLIC LIBRARY.

Atheneum Books for Young Readers
An imprint of Simon & Schuster Children's Publishing Division
1230 Avenue of the Americas
New York, New York 10020

Book design by Nina Barnett
The text of this book is set in Century Old Style.
First Edition
Printed in Singapore
10 9 8 7 6 5 4 3 2 1

Library of Congress Cataloging-in-Publication Data
Quarterbacks! Eighteen of Football's Greatest/ George
Sullivan.—1st ed.
p.   cm.
Summary: Profiles some of the top-rated quarterbacks of all time,
including Sammy Baugh, Bart Starr, Fran Tarkenton, Dan Marino,
Steve Young, and Troy Aikman.
ISBN 0-689-81334-1
1. Football players—United States—Biography—Juvenile
literature.
2. Football players—Rating of—United States—Juvenile literature.
3. Quarterback (Football)—Juvenile literature. [1. Football
Players.]
I. Title.
GV939.A1S92   1998
796.332'092'273—dc21 [B]
97-34167   CIP   AC

Contents

In the game's early days, when the football was more rounded and difficult to throw, the offense featured running. *(New York Public Library)*

Introduction

In football, the quarterback is king, no doubt about it. He handles the ball on virtually every play. He calls the signals and often the plays in the huddle.

Pass or run? It's up to the quarterback. He's the man in charge out there.

If it's a pass, once the ball has been snapped the quarterback has to choose from as many as three or four options, checking the coverage on each receiver and picking the right one. And he has to be able to do it in less time than it took you to read this paragraph.

Being a quarterback is the most demanding job in football, maybe in all of sports. To fulfill his role, a quarterback has to have good size, a strong arm, and a rocket release.

Today's quarterback has to have mobility, too, be a scrambler. Indeed, being agile is probably more important today than ever before. That's because pro defenses have reached a point where the quarterback can be pressured from every position, even safety and cornerback.

The result is that "the pocket" has become a danger zone. Broken ribs and bruised sternums are common. The concussion is no longer a rarity. A quarterback has to be tough enough to take hit after hit.

Of course, the ability to move around is not just a matter of self-preservation. Quarterbacks such as Brett Favre of the Packers and Mark Brunell of the Jaguars use their mobility to buy time for their receivers to work free against defensive players.

But Favre and Brunell not only throw on the run, they run on the run. They don't hesitate to dive for key third-down yardage to keep drives going or carry the ball on option plays at the goal line. Steve Young of the 49ers and John Elway of the Broncos also played the game that way.

Besides the ability to be elusive, a quarterback has to have intelligence, the ability to lead, and courage. Having the guts to hang in there in the face of an awesome pass rush is sometimes just as important as a strong throwing arm, perhaps even more important. More about courage later.

The role of the quarterback keeps growing in importance. "When I played, the media and the public pressure weren't there," Tom Flores, quarterback for the Oakland Raiders in the 1960s and the team's coach in the 1990s, told *Sports Illustrated.* "You just went out and played football.

"Today, when you're a first-round quarterback, you have to walk on water. You have to be a savior."

It wasn't always this way. In the early days, football was a running game. One problem was the football itself. During the 1920s, the ball had much

Many of today's quarterbacks don't hesitate to throw on the run or carry the ball. This is Brett Favre of the Packers. *(Wide World)*

more of a melon shape than it does today, and was difficult to grip. If the quarterback tried to throw, he had to kind of lob the ball. To pass was to gamble. The quarterback was just another member of the backfield.

The NFL began making the ball slimmer during the 1930s. The ball of the 1920s had a 23-inch girth (or what is technically called the "short circumference"). This was reduced by a half inch in 1931, and by a full inch in 1934.

With such a ball—21 1/4 to 21 1/2 inches in girth (its size today)—it was easier to get a firm grip. You could drill the ball with speed and accuracy.

Sammy Baugh, who joined the Washington Redskins in 1937 fresh out of Texas Christian University, took advantage of the rule change and, with his strong arm, launched a new era in pro football.

As a rookie, Baugh quarterbacked the Redskins to the Eastern Division title, then faced the Chicago Bears at Wrigley Field on a frigid December afternoon. On the first play from scrimmage, the ball on the Redskins' 9-yard line, Baugh

fired a quick pass to half-back Cliff Battles for a 43-yard gain.

It was almost unheard of for a quarterback to pass from inside his own 30-yard line in those days. That Baugh would do it from his end zone stunned the Bears. The Redskins went on to win the game and the title, 28–21, on the strength of four Baugh touchdown passes.

In the seasons after, Baugh kept demonstrating that the forward pass was a very efficient way to score a touchdown. Baugh's Redskins won the Eastern Division title five times and the NFL championship twice in Baugh's first 10 years with the team.

Fans were awed by Baugh's quick release. "He hardly ever looked at his receiver," Sid Luckman, who quarterbacked the Chicago Bears, once noted. "He cut loose the ball so quickly that opposing linemen seldom had a chance to smear him or force him to hurry his passing."

By the time "Slingin' Sam" retired in 1952, to pass was routine and the quarterback was a glamour figure.

The introduction of the T formation also boosted the quarterback's role. In the mid-1930s, most teams operated out of what was called the single wing, which looked something like the shotgun formation of the present day. The ball was snapped to a tailback or a fullback, both of whom were stationed several yards behind the center.

With the single wing, teams ran mostly running plays, using sweeps to either side, slants off tackle, or reverses. Plays developed very slowly and there was little chance for deception. Long runs and long passes were rare.

The T formation made a world of difference. The quarterback was set right behind the center. After taking the snap, he turned, concealing the ball. He then could hand off to a running back, pitch to a back, or keep the ball and pass to one of a variety of receivers.

The T formation, by putting the emphasis on quickness and deception, changed football for all time. All of today's pro teams use one of countless variations of the T.

When quarterback Sid Luckman reported to the Chicago Bears in the fall of 1939, his arrival coincided with owner George Halas's plan to install the T. Behind Luckman, whom Halas called the "perfect quarterback," the Bears swept to five Western Division and four league championships.

Luckman and Baugh took part in many legendary duels. Luckman, the deft ball handler, specialized in soft tosses to his backs and men in motion. Baugh was the more classic passer, standing erect, searching downfield, throwing bullet passes with the whiplike motion of his arm.

The tradition of outstanding quarterbacks—quarterbacks who take on a central role for the team—began with Sammy Baugh and Sid Luckman. Others quickly appeared—Otto Graham and Bobby Layne among them.

A few words about pro football's structure. From 1933 until its merger with the All-America Football Conference (AAFC) in 1949, teams in the National Football League (NFL) were divided into the Eastern and Western Divisions. The two division titlists met for the league championship.

After the merger, teams were assigned not to divisions, but to conferences, the American Conference and National Conference, and the two conference champions played for the league title. More changes came in 1967 after the league expanded and the conferences were subdivided into divisions.

The year 1967 is also important because that's the year that the NFL merged with the American Football League (AFL). Beginning with that merger, the two conference champions faced each other in what was called the World Championship Game, which, in 1970, came to be called the Super Bowl. Super Bowl V in 1971, incidentally, was the first to be identified by a Roman numeral.

Quarterbacking got another big boost in 1949 with the advent of free substitution. This permitted coaches to develop separate "platoons" of players, one for defense, one for offense. The era of the specialist was at hand. Like other of the game's offensive and defensive personnel, quarterbacks could work exclusively on developing the skills the position demanded.

Of course, not even the greatest quarterback can make a team successful by himself. He needs an offensive line that gives him the time to set up and pick out a target. He needs a strong running game to keep the defense honest. He needs fast, sure-handed receivers. And he needs a defensive team that keeps the opposing team from scoring and gets him the ball as much as possible.

In choosing which quarterbacks to profile in this book, statistics were looked upon with skepticism. Statistics can mislead, football statistics especially.

One example: John Elway of the Denver Broncos was arguably the most physically gifted athlete ever to play in the NFL. But only at random times in his career did Elway distinguish himself from a statistical standpoint. That's because Dan Reeves, coach of the Broncos during Elway's first

Joe Montana of the 49ers and Dan Marino of the Dolphins typified the elite quarterbacks of recent decades. *(Wide World)*

decade with the team, often kept him on a short leash, that is, played a ball-control offense and limited the number of passes he could throw.

After Reeves left Denver in 1992, Elway became a statistical sensation overnight. He led the NFL in attempts, completions, and passing yardage in 1993, and his rating as a passer zoomed to 92.8, marking the first time he had ever gotten into the 90s. (Passer ratings are based on a complicated formula devised by the NFL that involves percentage of completions, percentage of touchdown passes, percentage of interceptions, and the average gain per pass attempt.)

Elway was no more talented in 1993 than he was in 1992. What did change was Denver's offensive philosophy. Simply stated, Elway was given more of an opportunity to throw the ball.

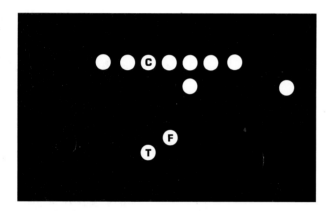

(Above) In the single-wing formation, center (C) snapped the ball back between his legs to one of two deep backs, the tailback (T) or fullback (F).

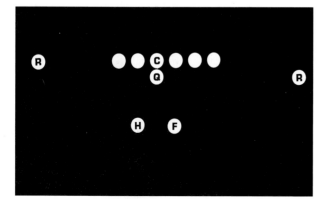

In choosing the quarterbacks featured here, one standard was applied. Imagine it's the Super Bowl, with two minutes remaining, and your team needs a touchdown to win.

Whom would you choose to quarterback the team?

Any one of the quarterbacks profiled in this book could do the job. Each could bring his team down the field under pressure.

A number of years ago, the San Diego Chargers hired Dr. Arnold J. Mandell, chairman of the Department of Psychiatry at the University of California, San Diego, to study the team and the behavior of its players. Out of the research, it was thought, Dr. Mandell might be able to determine what it takes to produce a winning edge.

Dr. Mandell observed the San Diego players at team meetings, in the dressing room, and from the sidelines during practices and games. He conducted some 200 interviews with team members. He later published his findings in an article in *Saturday Review/World.*

Concerning quarterbacks, Dr. Mandell said: "To stand there to the last millisecond, waiting for your receiver to reach the place the ball is supposed to go while you are being rushed by mammoth lineman—that takes sheer courage."

Courage is essential. Of Johnny Unitas, Merlin Olsen, defensive tackle of the Rams, once said, "You can't intimidate him. When he sees us coming he knows it's going to hurt and we know it's going to hurt, but he just stands there and takes it."

But it goes beyond mere courage, said Dr. Mandell. Top quarterbacks have what he called a "super-arrogance," an absolute belief in their skills. That's one of their strongest assets. Good quarterbacks know they're good.

(Left) In the T formation, the quarterback (Q) is positioned just behind the center (C). Pass receivers (R) are set wide on either side of the line. The deep backs, the halfback (H) and fullback (F, now called running backs), can also be used as receivers.

Brett Favre

Born: October 10, 1969;
Pass Christian, Mississippi
Height: 6'2"   Weight: 220
High School: Hancock North Central
(Pass Christian) High School
College: University of Southern Mississippi
Pro Teams: Atlanta Falcons, 1991;
Green Bay Packers, 1992–

The Green Bay Packers say that they aren't retiring any more jerseys. Well, some time in the next few years the chances are good the club will have to change its mind.

The reason is a fresh-faced quarterback with a cannon arm, the fastest release in the game, and a talent for scrambling and throwing that drives opposing defenses crazy.

The league's back-to-back MVP in 1995 and 1996, Brett Favre steered the Packers to a victory over the scrappy New England Patriots in Super Bowl XXXI in 1997 with two long touchdown passes and a scramble for another score. To master sportscaster John Madden, he was the game's most valuable player.

The Favre legend got off to an awkward start. As a fifth-grader on a team coached by his dad, Favre (rhymes with carve) played wide receiver.

In his first start, he caught a pass, fell on the ball, and had the wind knocked out of him. With Brett stretched out, crying, his dad raced out onto the field. "Get up, you baby," he said.

When Brett protested that he didn't want to play

When Favre scrambles, he's usually trying to set up a pass. *(Wide World)*

wide receiver anymore, his father put him at quarterback. Brett threw for two touchdowns and ran for two that afternoon.

"I knew this was the position for me," Favre recently told *Sport.* "The cheerleaders were cheering and the fans were yelling, and afterward I felt like, man, I'm really good."

At Southern Miss, it was more of the same. Favre led the underdog Golden Eagles to stunning wins over such powerhouses as Florida State, Alabama, and Auburn.

The Atlanta Falcons chose Favre in the second round of the 1991 draft. Like most rookie quarterbacks in the NFL, he spent the season on the bench. He threw only five passes, completing none.

The Packers, who had been impressed by Favre's exploits at Southern Miss, had been keeping close tabs on him. In January 1992, they gave up a first draft choice to land him.

The idea was for Favre to back up starter Don Majkowski. But when Majkowski sprained an ankle early in 1992, the 22-year-old Favre took over. He completed 64 percent of his passes that season and established himself as a fiery leader.

But 1993 was a struggle. The Packers had 34 turnovers that season, and Favre was responsible for 30 of them, including 24 interceptions. The problem was that Favre was too wild, too unpredictable. He liked to run around a lot and was guilty of some really weird throws. If a receiver was

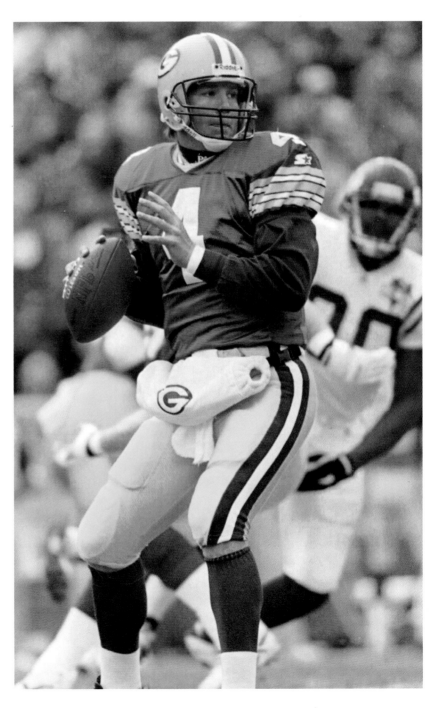

During 1995 and 1996, Favre passed for a league-leading 8,042 yards and 77 touchdowns. *(Wide World)*

Favre's early years with the Packers were often marked by frustration. *(Wide World)*

covered, he'd sometimes throw as hard as he could, hoping the ball would bounce off someone's helmet into the hands of some teammate.

Mike Holmgren, Green Bay's demanding coach, who had been an assistant with the San Francisco 49ers, wanted a quarterback more like Joe Montana, calm and efficient, an artist at picking apart defenses and directing long, relentless drives. Favre's frantic style didn't fit that image.

But Holmgren made up his mind to stick with Favre. His patience was rewarded. Favre eventually settled down and stopped trying to force things.

But he didn't stop being inventive. He still scrambles. With Favre calling plays, the defense can never relax.

In 1994, Favre led the Packers to a wild-card slot in the playoffs. A loss to Dallas ended the team's Super Bowl dreams, but Favre had set the stage for the years of greatness that were to come.

In 1995, Favre threw for a league-leading 4,413 yards and a team record 38 touchdowns, with only 13 interceptions. In the divisional playoffs, Favre coolly guided the Packers to a 27–17 upset of the Super Bowl champion San Francisco 49ers, which Favre called "the biggest win I ever had."

In the conference title match, after a slow start, Favre managed to steer the team into a 27–24 lead. But late in the game he threw a disastrous interception that helped the Cowboys pull ahead and win.

The crushing defeat caused the Packers to redouble their efforts. Before the season opened, however, the team was dealt a heavy blow when Favre revealed he was addicted to a painkilling drug and was entering a treatment center. He had started 63 consecutive games for the Packers and had come to be known as a player who refused to allow an injury to keep him from playing.

Favre kicked the painkiller habit and, once the season opened, helped spark the Packers to one impressive win after another. Again the Packers were division champs and again Favre was the league's MVP. This time they did not stumble, scoring a convincing victory over the Carolina Panthers in the conference championship.

In Super Bowl XXXI, Favre was masterful. Both of his touchdown throws came on audibles, that is, after he had sized up the Patriots' defense and called adjustments at the line of scrimmage. His 81-yard pass to a streaking Antonio Freeman was the longest touchdown from scrimmage in Super Bowl history. The Packers won, 35–21.

The Green Bay Packers had won Super Bowls I and II under the legendary Vince Lombardi in 1967 and 1968. Twenty-nine years went by before the team got to play in Super Bowl XXXI. And, led by Favre, they made a repeat visit in 1998, when they lost in a close match against John Elway and the Denver Broncos.

Bart Starr. Ray Nitschke. Don Hutson. They are some of Green Bay's all-time greats. In a ceremony at Lambeau Field one cold winter afternoon, Brett Favre's name is likely to be added to that list and his number 4 jersey put into retirement.

The ceremony won't be anything new for the quarterback his teammates call "Country." Two of his previous uniforms—from high school and Southern Miss—have already been retired.

Favre has one of the fastest releases in the NFL. It's been timed at 1.6 seconds.
(Wide World)

Troy Aikman

Born: November 21, 1966   West Covina, California
Height: 6'4"   Weight: 220
High School: Henryetta (Oklahoma) High School
Colleges: University of Oklahoma, UCLA
Team: Dallas Cowboys, 1989–

Troy Aikman's extraordinary football success, which includes three Super Bowl wins, plus his movie-star name and good looks, makes him what his agent calls a "marketing dream." But Aikman is often uncomfortable with all the attention he gets. He prefers a plain and quiet life. During football season, he shops at 1 A.M. and has pizza delivered to his home three or four times a week so he won't have to face autograph seekers.

The youngest of three children, Troy was born and raised in suburban Los Angeles. When he was 12, the family moved to Henryetta, a small town in Oklahoma, where the Aikmans bought a ranch and raised cattle, pigs, and chickens.

At first, Troy didn't like Oklahoma. "We had no neighbors," he says.

But he later came to enjoy country life. He wore boots and western clothes and enjoyed country

Recruited by the University of Oklahoma out of high school, the rangy, strong-armed Aikman switched to UCLA because the team stressed the passing game. *(Wide World)*

9

Aikman scrambles but can't escape Mike Pitts of the Eagles. *(Wide World)*

music. When he got to be old enough, he drove a pickup.

He recalls being a "real dorky kid" in high school who once enrolled in a typing class with 38 girls.

Today, Aikman sponsors a scholarship program at Henryetta High School and provides funds for a fitness center for local schools. In appreciation, the town has named a street after him.

Following a glittering career as a high school quarterback, Aikman went on to the University of Oklahoma. But the Oklahoma team, coached by Barry Switzer, planned to stress the running game. The rocket-armed Aikman quickly transferred to UCLA (University of California, Los Angeles).

There, leading an offense that stressed passing, he enjoyed two banner seasons.

In April 1989, Dallas picked Aikman in the NFL draft. He was the first player to be chosen that year. The Cowboy team, with a new owner and a new coach, was a team in turmoil.

Playing behind a leaky offensive line, Aikman endured one battering after another. He started 11 games; he lost 11. "The worst season of my life," he calls it.

In 1991, the Cowboys installed a quick-release passing game that took advantage of Aikman's strengths—his compact throwing motion and his ability to spot secondary receivers when his primary receiver is covered. However, a knee injury knocked Aikman out for much of the season.

In 1992, with Aikman injury-free, the Cowboys cruised to the championship of the National Football Conference. In Super Bowl XXVII against the Buffalo Bills, Aikman was as good as he's ever been, firing four touchdown passes in the Cowboys' 52–17 blowout.

"At some point in the second quarter," Aikman said after, "I felt I had control of the ball game. And when I really get on a roll throwing the ball, I feel like I'm going to complete every pass I throw." Aikman's brilliance that day earned him the Super Bowl Most Valuable Player award.

The very next season the Cowboys landed in the Super Bowl a second time against the Bills. Again the Cowboys prevailed, 30–13. With the victory, Aikman became the fifth quarterback in history to win back-to-back Super Bowls.

Injuries hampered the Cowboys in their efforts to win three straight Super Bowls. But 1995, with Barry Switzer as the new head coach, was another championship year. By upending the Steelers in Super Bowl XXX, Aikman and the Cowboys won their third championship in four years, a feat no other team has accomplished.

Aikman, a bachelor, relaxes by listening to country music, dialing up his E-mail, and socializing with friends. He was once asked his reaction to being named one of *People* magazine's "fifty most beautiful people." "Well," he said, "they must not know very many people."

"Most of Aikman's passes are perfect throws," sportscaster John Madden once observed. *(Wide World)*

Aikman had plenty to celebrate during his career, including three Super Bowl wins. *(Wide World)*

Steve Young

Born: October 11, 1961   Salt Lake City, Utah
Height: 6'2"   Weight: 200
High School: Greenwich (Connecticut) High School
College: Brigham Young University
Teams: Los Angeles Express (USFL), 1984–1985; Tampa Bay Buccaneers, 1985–1986; San Francisco 49ers, 1987–

The Super Bowl often proves to be a lopsided affair, and Super Bowl XXIX in 1995 was no exception. Final score: San Francisco 49ers 49, San Diego Chargers 26.

But never has a mismatch developed with such suddenness. Led by 33-year-old Steve Young, a scrambler and the NFL's leading passer, the 49ers struck early and often, bewildering the San Diego defense.

After the opening kickoff return, it took only three plays for Young to get the 49ers into the end zone. He topped off the drive with a 44-yard touchdown pass to wide receiver Jerry Rice.

The three-play sequence took one minute, 24 seconds. It is the fastest touchdown in Super Bowl history.

The next time the 49ers got the ball, Young produced a replay, moving the team 79 yards in just four plays. The drive included a 21-yard scramble by Young and was crowned by his 51-yard touchdown pass to running back Ricky Watters.

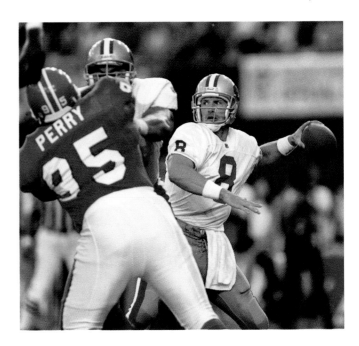

Young was consistently one of the NFL's leading passers; twice he won MVP honors. *(Wide World)*

Sometimes Young scrambled to buy time, but he also ranked as one of San Francisco's leading rushers. *(Wide World)*

The 49ers had a 14–0 lead in less than five minutes. No one had the slightest doubt about the outcome.

For Steve Young, Super Bowl XXIX was a great personal triumph. With a record six touchdown passes and 49 yards rushing (to lead all of the game's rushers), Young earned the Super Bowl's Most Valuable Player award.

That was only part of it. Ever since he had arrived in San Francisco in 1987, Young had operated in the shadow of the legendary Joe Montana, who had been a fixture with the 49ers for 14 seasons and had steered the team to four—yes, *four!*—Super Bowl victories.

Montana's fans resented Young. They said that he was weak in clutch situations and that the only reason he ran with the ball was because he couldn't read defenses. They said that he had trouble with passes in the flat and didn't see the entire field as well as Montana could. They pointed out that he was left-handed, and said a lefty quarterback can't win in the NFL.

Super Bowl XXIX stilled the critics. No longer was Steve Young to be haunted by the ghost of Joe Montana.

Young took a long and winding road to get to San

Francisco. He was brought up in a Mormon household in Greenwich, Connecticut, where his parents had settled. After high school, he enrolled at Brigham Young University in Provo, Utah.

By his senior year, 1983, Steve was arguably the best of all college quarterbacks, although he was the runner-up in the voting for the Heisman Trophy, which goes to the year's outstanding collegiate player. After college, Steve sidestepped the NFL to join the Los Angeles Express of the new United States Football League (USFL), signing what was said to be the richest contract in the history of team sports up to that time.

But the USFL folded after two years. Steve then landed with the NFL's Tampa Bay Buccaneers. The Tampa Bay coaching staff wanted a drop-back passer, not a scrambler. They didn't know how to use Steve. After two dismal seasons, he was traded to the 49ers.

Several seasons as Joe Montana's understudy followed. When he finally got a chance to take over the team, Young was brilliant.

Not only did he prove to be a master of the short passing game, he was also a constant long-ball threat. Between 1991 and 1996, he won the league's passing title five times. In 1992, he was named the NFL's Most Valuable Player.

Young's league-leading completion percentage of 70.3 in 1994 broke the club record held by Montana. Young also set an NFL quarterback-rating record of 112.8 that season, breaking another of Montana's marks. For his dazzling perfor-

mance, Young received his second MVP award.

Young (unlike Montana) was a gutsy and determined runner, always willing to take a vicious shot or two for an extra couple of yards. This habit led to some impressive yardage totals and a long list of injuries.

After he suffered bruised ribs, a groin pull, and two concussions in 1996, people close to Young suggested he might want to think about quitting. But Young made it clear he had no retirement plans. He was focused on getting to the Super Bowl again—and no one will be surprised if he does.

Young tunes up his arm for the second half of Super Bowl XXIX at Miami's Joe Robbie Stadium. *(Wide World)*

John Elway

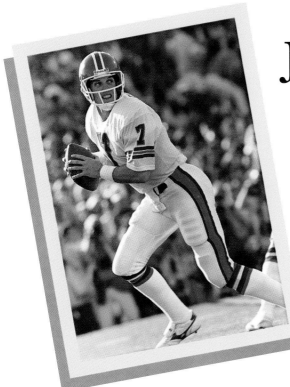

Born: June 28, 1960   Port Angeles, Washington
Height: 6'3"   Weight: 210
High School: Granada Hills (California) High School
College: Stanford University
Team: Denver Broncos, 1983–

Pro football history is loaded with tales of dramatic game-winning touchdown drives. Johnny Unitas marching the Colts to the NFL title against the Giants in sudden death in 1958. Joe Montana taking the San Francisco 49ers 89 yards in the final minutes of the 1981 conference title game against the Cowboys to earn the 49ers their first trip to the Super Bowl.

John Elway has had games like those, lots of them. The most notable came on a bitter cold January afternoon in 1986 in Cleveland when the Broncos confronted the Browns. The AFC championship was at stake.

The Broncos seemed dead. Trailing by seven points with five minutes, 32 seconds remaining, they had the ball on their own 2-yard line. The Cleveland end zone was 98 yards away.

In the huddle, Elway smiled. "If you work hard," he said, "good things are going to happen."

On first down, Elway passed for a short gain, then scrambled for the first down. Another pass got

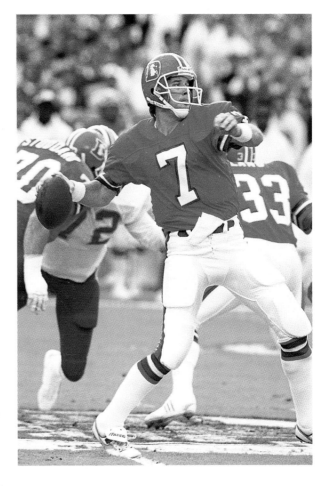

For ten of his NFL seasons, Elway passed for 3,000 or more yards. (*Wide World*)

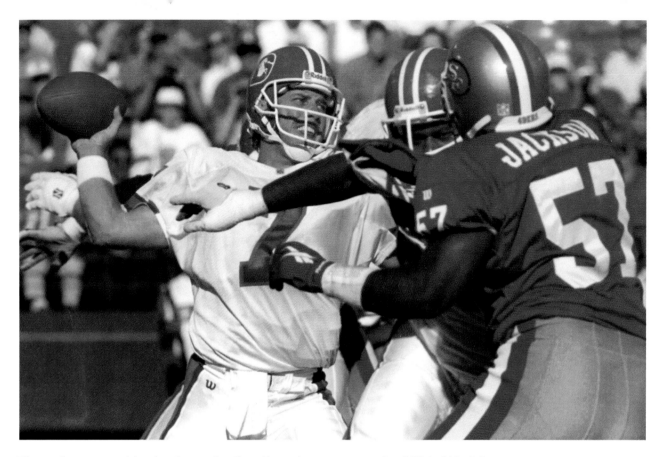

Elway keeps cool in the face of a San Francisco pass rush. *(Wide World)*

22 yards. He followed with a 12-yarder.

Shortly after, however, Elway and the Broncos faced a third-and-18 situation. Firing from a shotgun formation, he came through with a 20-yard completion for a first down on the Cleveland 28. After a 14-yard throw, Elway ran for 9 yards to the 5-yard line.

From there, he nailed the touchdown pass that sent the game into overtime. A field goal following two long Elway passes won it for the Broncos.

Cleveland fans were in shock. It was "the kind of game you dream about," Elway said.

For a decade and a half, John Elway worked such miracles for the Denver Broncos. He became the king of fourth-quarter comeback victories, chalking up 41 of them (through 1996).

Elway's will to win, to never give up, combined with his strong arm, deft touch, and a willingness to scramble, helped to make the Broncos the No. 1 team in the American Football Conference during big chunks of the 1980s and 1990s, and earned the team four trips to the Super Bowl.

The Broncos managed to win only one of those games, Super Bowl XXXII, a thriller against the Packers. Before that victory Elway maintained a level head about the losses. "There's something to be said for just *getting* to three Super Bowls," he would say. "How many guys never got there?"

Tall, strong, with big hands and long legs, young John Elway was encouraged and instructed in sports by his father, a college football coach. In high school, John was a straight-A student and starred in three sports. At Stanford, he was an All-America quarterback and runner-up in the Heisman Trophy voting in 1982.

The Colts, who drafted Elway, traded him to the Broncos, where he was made the starting quarterback by coach Dan Reeves. Elway had a rocky rookie season. He was criticized for throwing into coverage, believing that his powerful arm could get the ball to the receiver even if he wasn't open.

But, eventually, the Broncos began to win consistently under Elway's leadership. In his first decade with the team, he carried Denver to four AFC championships, with an 89–46–1 regular-season record.

This was despite the fact that the Denver system never put great emphasis on passing. Coach Reeves, with whom Elway had a frosty relationship, preferred a conservative approach. Elway would throw long only once or twice a half, or when the Broncos had fallen behind. Then his powerful right arm would be unleashed to produce a game-saving drive or two.

In 1996, with Mike Shanahan coaching, the 36-year-old Elway was still scrambling and making clutch plays. More precise and efficient than he had ever been, he steered the Broncos to the best record in the AFC that season. But in the playoffs, Elway was blitzed into defeat by the Jacksonville Jaguars.

That same year, 1996, Elway signed a new five-year contract with the Broncos. It guaranteed him that he would end his career with the team. His teammates and many thousands of Denver fans are glad of that, especially now that they have that Super Bowl win.

Elway launches a pass during a practice session for Super Bowl XXIV in New Orleans. The Broncos got buried by the 49ers, 55–10. (Wide World)

Elway gets sacked by George Martin of the New York Giants during Super Bowl XXI at the Rose Bowl in Pasadena, California, in 1987. The Giants won, 39–20. (Wide World)

Dan Marino

Born: September 15, 1961
Pittsburgh, Pennsylvania
Height: 6'4"   Weight: 220
High School: Central Catholic (Pittsburg) High School
College: University of Pittsburgh
Team: Miami Dolphins, 1983–

Each year on the Saturday morning before the Super Bowl, the selectors for the Pro Football Hall of Fame gather to decide which candidates will be enshrined the following summer. Sometime during the first decade of the 21st century, Dan Marino's name will appear on that list of candidates. (Retired players have to wait five years before they qualify for induction.)

Marino is a shoo-in for membership. Indeed, his place in the Hall of Fame was probably assured after the first decade or so of his career.

It's easy to understand why. With his strong right arm and superfast release, Marino helped shape the character of pro football as it's played today, switching the emphasis from the run to the pass.

And there are all those mind-boggling statistics. Marino holds just about every passing record of any significance, including those for career pass completions, passing yards, and touchdown passes. In 1996, he threw his 4,000th completion and surpassed 50,000 yards in total passing yardage.

Dan Marino has been tossing footballs around for as long as he can remember. His dad worked as a delivery-truck driver for a Pittsburgh newspaper, a job that left him free in the afternoons to play with his son. "He'd be waiting for me to get out of school," Marino once told *Inside Sports*. "Then we'd throw to each other the rest of the day."

In high school, Marino not only quarterbacked; he also punted and placekicked, and was a pitcher on the baseball team. His fastball was once clocked at 92 miles per hour, exceptional for a high schooler.

At the University of Pittsburgh, Marino put aside other sports to concentrate on football. There his quick release and supreme self-confidence became his trademarks.

In his junior year, Marino led Pitt to an 11–1 record. But 1982, his senior year, was something of a disappointment, for the team lost some games that it had been expected to win.

That's one reason why Marino wasn't thought of too highly by pro scouts. Five quarterbacks and a total of 26 players overall were selected ahead of Marino in the 1983 pro football draft.

Marino began his rookie season at Miami as back-up quarterback to Dave Woodley. But when Woodley played poorly in the first several games of the season, coach Don Shula replaced him with Marino.

Right from the start, Marino made the job of pro signal-caller look easy. Under his leadership, the team won every game but one. Marino captured the Rookie of the Year award and became the first rookie quarterback selected as a starter in the Pro Bowl.

The next season was even better. Marino set a helmetful of passing records—for touchdowns (48), passing yards (5,084), and completions (363). The Dolphins roared through the regular season, the playoffs, and into Super Bowl XIX. "His [Marino's] feats this season have left NFL coaches and players gasping in amazement," said *Newsday*.

Marino has absorbed more than his share of bumps and bruises. Here he is sacked by defensive end Marvin Washington of the New York Jets. *(Wide World)*

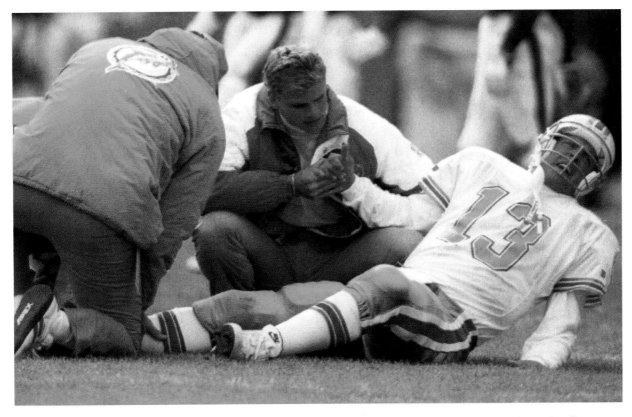

Marino grimaces in pain after suffering a torn Achilles tendon in a game against the Browns in 1993. The injury sidelined Marino for the season. *(Wide World)*

The Super Bowl pitted Marino and the Dolphins against Joe Montana's 49ers. San Francisco controlled matters that day, crushing the Dolphins, 38–16. Under pressure from the start, Marino was sacked four times, a high for the season, and forced into throwing two interceptions. Afterward, Marino could afford to shrug. He was only 23. He figured there would be more Super Bowls.

And indeed Marino continued to shine. Each year he produced awesome statistics and registered a few more milestones. But there was no championship.

Then in a regular-season game against the Browns in 1993, Marino suffered a devastating injury, rupturing his right Achilles tendon. After 145 consecutive starts, Marino was out of the lineup. Months and months of grueling rehabilitation followed.

A number of leg operations—eight in all—cut his mobility. A broken ankle in 1996 added another bump in the road.

From each setback, Marino returned with more determination than ever to win the prize that had eluded him. He sensed that his ranking as a quarterback would be determined by what his team did, or failed to do.

In 1996, Jimmy Johnson, who had won two Super Bowls as coach of the Dallas Cowboys, took over in Miami, replacing Shula. Marino liked the challenge of working with a new coach. In an early meeting

Thanks to his strong right arm and lightning release, Marino owns practically every major passing record. *(Wide World)*

with Johnson, he told him that he didn't care if he threw only 10 passes a game, all he wanted to do was win—win the Super Bowl, that is.

Jim Kelly

Born: February 14, 1960
East Brady, Pennsylvania
Height: 6'3"   Weight: 225
High School: East Brady High School
College: University of Miami
Teams: Houston Gamblers (USFL), 1984–1985;
Buffalo Bills, 1986–1996

The first time the Buffalo Bills sought to sign Jim Kelly, he rejected their offers, saying, "You can't be a great quarterback in the snow and 30-mile-an-hour wind." Three years later, in 1986, when the Bills came calling a second time, Kelly listened, eventually signing a contract that made him the highest-paid player in pro football history up to that time.

For 11 seasons beginning in 1986, the smart and elusive Kelly, directing an exciting, fast-striking no-huddle offense, reigned not merely as a standout quarterback but as a unique model.

Kelly's success is plain to see. For four consecutive seasons beginning in 1991, Kelly led the Bills to the Super Bowl, an incredible feat. Unfortunately, he has no Super Bowl ring to show for his efforts.

From western Pennsylvania, a territory that has produced such elite quarterbacks as Johnny Unitas, Joe Namath, Joe Montana, and Dan Marino, Kelly and his five brothers were encouraged by their father to play sports. Young Jimmy seemed to have special gifts. When he was eight years old, he could already throw a spiral pass.

Injuries hobbled Kelly late in his career and helped lead to his retirement in 1996.
(Wide World)

In 1984 and 1985, Kelly established his greatness while quarterbacking for the Houston Gamblers of the United States Football League. *(Wide World)*

In high school, Kelly became a legend. As a senior, he was the all-conference punter, placekicker, safety, quarterback, and player of the year. The school retired his jersey number after he graduated.

Heavily recruited by college teams, Kelly chose the University of Miami. Quarterbacking a pass-oriented offense, he helped to turn the lowly Hurricanes into a national football power.

Kelly was disappointed when he was drafted by the Buffalo Bills, and not just because of the snow and the cold. The Bills were a hapless team, struggling to win as many games as they lost.

Fate took a hand. Kelly received an offer from the Houston Gamblers of the struggling United States Football League. League officials hoped that Kelly would draw the kind of attention that Joe Namath had attracted for the American Football League a couple of decades before.

Kelly was a sensation with the Gamblers, putting up incredible numbers. As the quarterback for a wide-open passing attack, using four wide receivers, Kelly, as a rookie, passed for an amazing 44 touchdowns and an equally amazing 5,219 yards. A knee injury the next year cooled him off a bit. But in his two USFL seasons, Kelly was arguably the best quarterback in professional football (although some critics said he hadn't faced defenses equal to those in the NFL).

The USFL collapsed in 1985 and released its players. Kelly then signed a record five-year, $8 million contract with the Bills.

Kelly was looked upon as a savior in Buffalo.

Kelly rejoices after a Bills touchdown in Super Bowl XXV against the New York Giants. But the Giants went on to win, handing Kelly the first of his four Super Bowl defeats. *(Wide World)*

Ticket sales boomed. But he was no magician. It took several seasons before the Bills became contenders. The addition of the no-huddle "hurry-up" offense helped, with Kelly announcing each play at the line of scrimmage. The speed with which the Bills could rip off a sequence of plays often unnerved the opposition and threw off their timing.

By 1990, the Bills were the dominant team in the AFC and Kelly was being hailed as the NFL's best quarterback. The Bills breezed through the playoffs that year and were favored to beat the New York Giants in Super Bowl XXV.

They came very close. In the game's final minutes, Kelly marched the Bills down the field. On the last play of the game, a Buffalo field goal attempt drifted just wide. The Bills lost, 20–19.

Kelly and the Bills figured they would get back to the Super Bowl, and they were right. Their sad loss to the Giants in 1991 was the first of four consecutive Super Bowl appearances— and defeats. In 1992 and 1993, the Bills were simply blown away, first by the Redskins, and then by the Cowboys. In Super Bowl XXVIII against the Cowboys in 1994, Buffalo was leading, 13–6, as the third quarter began. But a Thurman Thomas fumble and, later, an interception led to Dallas touchdowns and a 30–13 win for the Cowboys.

Kelly retired after the season of 1996. Fans in Buffalo remember him for the precise way he ran the team's explosive no-huddle offense. They remember him for his resilience, the way he would bounce back from a defeat, and for taking the Bills to the Super Bowl four years in a row. They remember his work for the Bills' organization and the community.

Sure, the Bills lost four Super Bowls. But in Buffalo they don't blame Jim Kelly for that.

Joe Montana

Born: June 11, 1956
Monongahela, Pennsylvania
Height: 6'2"   Weight: 195
High School: Ringgold High School
(Monongahela)
College: University of Notre Dame
Teams: San Francisco 49ers, 1979–1992;
Kansas City Chiefs, 1993–1994

To this day, he is an icon in San Francisco, where he led the 49ers to four Super Bowl victories in 11 seasons and established himself as the finest quarterback of his era, and perhaps any era.

The numbers say it all: 16 NFL seasons, 40,551 passing yards, 273 touchdown passes, three Super Bowl MVP trophies, and two regular-season MVP awards.

Joe Cool, he was called, and no wonder. A master of the last-ditch drive, Montana led 31 fourth-quarter comeback victories for the 49ers.

When the San Francisco 49ers drafted Montana in 1979, they had their doubts about the skinny, slope-shouldered quarterback from Notre Dame. Both his ability to throw deep and his consistency were questioned. Other teams were just as skeptical. Montana wasn't picked until the third round, the 82nd player chosen.

There were complaints about his weak arm and lack of physical strength. Even as a kid, years before, they caused him to almost quit his midget

football team in Monongahela, Pennsylvania. But when his father heard of his plans, he told him, "Get your uniform because you're going back to practice. I don't care if you play or not, but you're going to practice." Joe's father didn't want his son to even *think* of quitting.

During his sophomore year at Notre Dame, the legend began to build. With the Irish trailing Air Force, 30–10, with 13 minutes to play, Montana engineered a 31–30 victory. In the Cotton Bowl, Houston led Notre Dame, 34–12, with less than eight minutes remaining; Montana turned on his magic, directing the Irish to a 35–34 win.

With the 49ers, Montana was allowed to develop gradually. But early in 1980, when he took over the quarterback position on a full-time basis, he impressed everyone with his efficiency and cool authority. In the final minutes of the 1981 NFC title game against the Dallas Cowboys, with the 49ers trailing by two points, Montana moved the offense 89 yards. The climax was a third-down, 6-yard pass that resulted in what is still referred to as "the Catch"—Dwight Clark's leaping end-zone grab. Moments later, a field goal won it for the 49ers.

Two weeks later in Super Bowl XVI, Montana guided the 49ers to their first championship, thus ending some 30 years of frustration. Montana returned three years later for Super Bowl XIX, this time outdueling Miami's Dan Marino, 38–16.

"The Catch" was one of the two greatest moments in Montana's career. The other came in Super Bowl XXIII in 1989. With three minutes, 10 seconds remaining, the 49ers trailed the Cincinnati Bengals, 16–13, and were 92 yards from the go-ahead touchdown.

In the last-ditch drive, Montana called only two running plays, and completed eight of nine passes. The crusher came with 39 seconds left and

Montana retired in 1994, ending his career in the uniform of the Kansas City Chiefs.
(Wide World)

Montana facing second-and-two at the 10-yard line.

The Bengal defense figured that Montana would be targeting Jerry Rice (who had caught 11 passes and would be named the game's MVP). They overlooked John Taylor, who lined up at tight end. Taylor headed straight for the end zone and was running at full speed when Montana hit him with the game winner.

Montana and the 49ers were back in the Super Bowl the very next year to face the Denver Broncos. Montana set a Super Bowl record that day by throwing five touchdown passes, and the 49ers romped, 55–10. Only one other quarterback, Terry Bradshaw of the Steelers, had won four Super Bowls.

Montana hoped to own five Super Bowl rings, but it never happened. He missed all of the season of 1991 and a big chunk of 1992 with injuries. He played his last two seasons with the Kansas City Chiefs.

At ceremonies in San Francisco announcing his retirement, more than 20,000 Montana worshipers were on hand. The mayor was there along with Montana's family, friends, and former teammates. Throughout the afternoon, Montana never showed any tears or signs of emotion. He was Joe Cool to the very end.

(Above) Montana goes to the air in the first half of Super Bowl XXIV against the Denver Broncos. Montana led the 49ers to a 55–10 win in what was his fourth Super Bowl victory. *(Wide World)*

(Left) Montana holds the all-time records for pass completions, yards gained, and TDs in playoff competition. *(Wide World)*

Terry Bradshaw

Born: September 2, 1948   Shreveport, Louisiana
Height: 6'3"   Weight: 210
High School: Woodlawn (Shreveport) High School
College: Louisiana Tech
Team: Pittsburgh Steelers, 1970–1983
Elected to the Hall of Fame in 1989

Terry Bradshaw had his neck broken during his playing days and it still gives him pain. His wrist was broken, too, and it never stops aching. He also has constant pain in his lower back. When Terry gets out of bed in the morning, he has to roll around on the floor for a few minutes to pop some of his body parts into place and get himself going.

The physical distress is only part of it. Bradshaw also sustained a fair amount of emotional pain during his career, especially during his early years; pain that was brought on by criticism and ridicule.

Bradshaw has learned to live with the physical pain. As for the criticism, he found a way to put an end to that, a method of getting the fans and media to give him some respect. He simply went out and won four Super Bowls.

Bradshaw arrived at the Steelers training camp from Louisiana Tech in 1970 with great expectations. Clean-cut and solidly built, he could throw the ball a mile. Said one scouting report: "Bradshaw has such a fabulous arm that you could charge admission to watch him warm up."

During Bradshaw's reign in Pittsburgh, the Steelers won eight division titles and four Super Bowls. *(Wide World)*

As a rookie in the Steelers lineup, Bradshaw endured a season that he himself has called a disaster. "I was totally unprepared for pro ball," he says. "I had had no schooling on reading defenses. I never studied the game films the way a quarterback should."

In addition, he threw the ball so hard his receivers often couldn't hold on to it. He ended up completing only 38 percent of his passes as a rookie.

And he got tagged by the media as not being very bright, what Bradshaw has called a "Dumb Image." Once, when he got hurt during a game, the crowd cheered. Bradshaw's confidence nosedived. By the end of the season, Bradshaw was on the bench and Notre Dame's Terry Hanratty was doing the quarterbacking.

In 1971, Bradshaw got his starting job back, and he was at the helm for all but one game in 1972. By now, Bradshaw was beginning to show some promise. In 1972, he guided the Steelers to their first divisional championship in 40 years of NFL competition. But in 1973, he suffered a separated shoulder that cut his playing time.

Things didn't really begin to change for Bradshaw until 1975, when he led the Steelers to a stunning win over Minnesota in Super Bowl IX. In 1976, he did it again, quarterbacking the Steelers to victory over the Cowboys in Super Bowl X.

The 1976 game did much to help still the criticism. In the face of a safety blitz, Bradshaw passed to Lynn Swann for 64 yards and a touchdown, a play that carried the Steelers to the championship.

Bradshaw hands off to running back Franco Harris during Super Bowl XIII against the Cowboys. The Steelers won, 35–31. *(Wide World)*

After the play, the blitzer smeared Bradshaw, who left the game with a concussion. Not only was Bradshaw a winner, he'd hang in there; he was a tough guy who took his hits. The Pittsburgh fans loved it.

It kept getting better. In Super Bowl XIII in 1979, Bradshaw passed for 300 yards for the first time in his career, as the Steelers overcame the Dallas Cowboys, 35–31. Bradshaw was named the game's Most Valuable Player.

Up to that time, no quarterback had ever won three Super Bowls. The next January, when Terry guided the Steelers to a win over the Los Angeles Rams in Super Bowl XIV, it was icing on the cake.

It was no easy win. The Rams led at halftime. In the third quarter, Terry hit John Stallworth with a pass that was good for 73 yards and a touchdown that boosted the Steelers into the lead. The game ended with the Steelers on top, 31–19. Again Bradshaw earned MVP honors.

What do four Super Bowl rings mean to Bradshaw? "They mean," he says, "that you've got it made."

Bradshaw was always popular with his team-mates and other players in the league. They liked his friendly, cheerful manner. After his playing days ended in 1983, Bradshaw brought those qualities to the television booth as a football analyst. But he feels his considerable television success is quite secondary to his football career. "Playing in the pros," he says, "that was the greatest, the best thing that happened to me."

In his early years with the Steelers, Bradshaw spent a good amount of time watching someone else do the quarter-backing. *(George Sullivan)*

Roger Staubach

Born: February 3, 1942   Cincinnati, Ohio
Height: 6'3"   Weight: 205
High School: Purcell (Cincinnati) High School
College: U.S. Naval Academy
Team: Dallas Cowboys, 1969–1979
Elected to the Hall of Fame in 1985

It seems strange now, in light of all their playoff victories and Super Bowl wins during the 1990s, but at one time the Dallas Cowboys were America's choke team. For a long stretch beginning in the late 1960s, the Cowboys lost almost every game that really mattered, including two NFL championships, two conference championships, and one Super Bowl. What made the situation even worse is that they were always favored.

Roger Staubach helped to turn things around. With his powerful arm—he threw a "hard" ball—and a tendency to scramble, to pull the ball down and suddenly charge up the middle or skirt an end, "Roger the Dodger," as he was sometimes called, showed the Dallas Cowboys how to win the big ones.

Roger Staubach began playing quarterback in high school, where he frequently ran option plays. Rolling out to either his right or left, Roger had the choice of keeping the ball and running, or passing. He was looked upon as a better runner than passer.

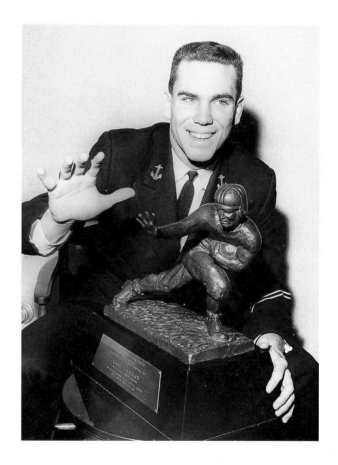

A graduate of the U.S. Naval Academy, Staubach, in 1985, became the first Heisman Trophy winner to be inducted into the Pro Football Hall of Fame. *(Wide World)*

Roger went on to the U.S. Naval Academy, where he won recognition as one of the outstanding collegiate players of all time. He was twice an All-America choice, and in 1963 he won the Heisman Trophy.

Although he was drafted by the Cowboys, Roger, as a graduate of the Naval Academy, was committed to navy service. The only uniforms he wore for the next four years were that of an ensign and later a lieutenant.

Roger reported to the Cowboys as a 27-year-old rookie in the summer of 1969. Craig Morton was the Dallas quarterback, and for a time he and Roger shared quarterbacking duties. But toward the end of the 1971 season, Roger became No. 1.

Staubach was spectacular as a starter. In the playoffs, he steered the Cowboys to decisive wins over the Minnesota Vikings and San Francisco 49ers to win the conference title. In Super Bowl VI, the Cowboys faced the Miami Dolphins. Roger's 7-yard scoring pass to Lance Alworth earned Dallas its first touchdown. Another 7-yarder, this one to Mike Ditka, put the game out of Miami's reach. The final score: Dallas 24, Miami 3. Roger, who completed 12 of 19 passes and rushed five times for 18 yards, was named the game's MVP.

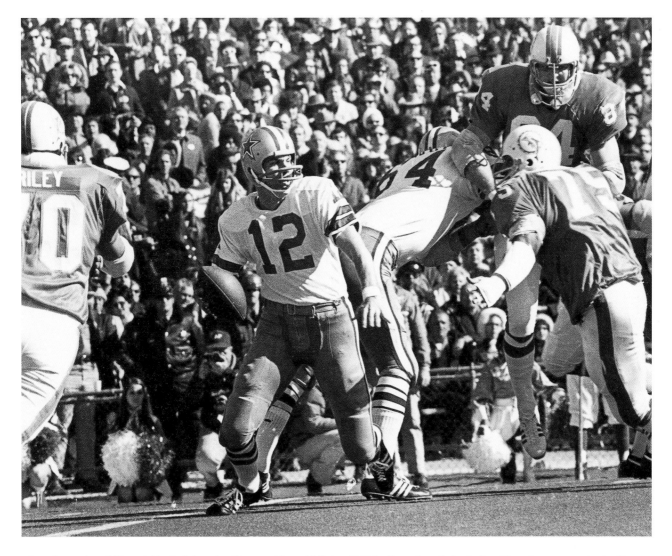

Against the Miami Dolphins in Super Bowl VI in 1972, Staubach led the Cowboys to their first - ever Super Bowl win. *(Wide World)*

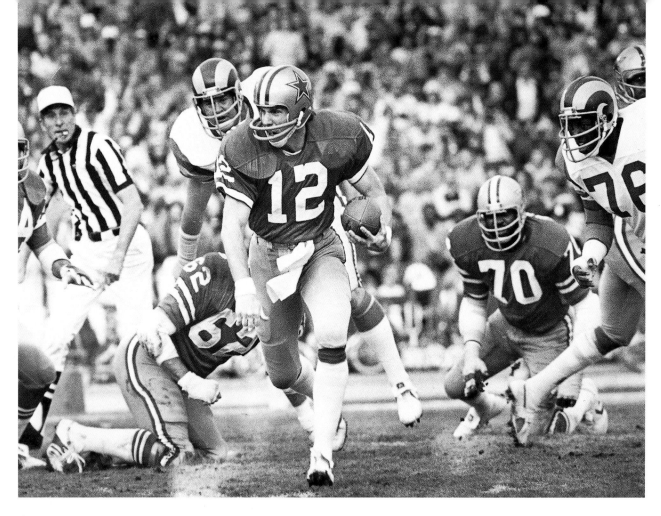

Staubach was a scrambler; "Roger the Dodger" he was called. *(Wide World)*

Roger was the Dallas quarterback throughout the rest of the 1970s. As the Cowboys' man in charge, he led the team to a stunning 85–30 record that included four conference championships and victories in Super Bowls VI and XII.

During his career, Roger often demonstrated an uncanny ability to lead the team in come-from-behind wins. Staubach rallied the Cowboys to no fewer than 23 fourth-quarter comebacks that ended in victory. Fourteen of them occurred in the game's final two minutes or overtime.

"I honestly used to feel sorry for the other team's defense," Cliff Harris, a Dallas safety, said, "watching Roger go to work in those last two minutes. There was really nothing you could do to stop him when he was on."

Long before his playing days ended, Staubach began preparing himself for a second career by working during the off-season for a commercial real estate firm in Dallas.

Upon retirement, he formed the Staubach Company, which today provides a wide range of services for companies that want to build or lease office or industrial space. There was a big problem at first. "You'd go to a meeting with possible clients and all they'd want to do was talk about sports," an employee recalled. Roger's company became a success, but he had to work hard to prove that he was an expert in something else besides quarterbacking.

Fran Tarkenton

Born: February 3, 1940   Richmond, Virginia
Height: 6'1"   Weight: 195
High School: Athens (Georgia) High School
College: University of Georgia
Teams: Minnesota Vikings, 1961–1966,
1972–1978; New York Giants, 1967–1971
Elected to the Hall of Fame in 1986

Fran Tarkenton didn't look like a pro quarterback. He wasn't especially tall and he didn't have a quick release or rifle arm. He didn't throw bullets; he threw rainbows.

And he didn't play the game the way most coaches thought it should be played. Tarkenton was a scrambler; he floated around the backfield. He was running-and-shooting a couple of decades before the strategy became common.

Once, in a game against the Los Angeles Rams, Tarkenton ducked, dodged, and retreated to a point more than 35 yards behind the line of scrimmage before getting the ball away. Another time, he scrambled for 28 seconds before passing.

For a quarterback who is usually remembered for running all over the field, Tarkenton compiled some incredible passing statistics. By the time he retired in 1978 after 18 NFL seasons, Tarkenton had thrown more footballs for more yardage, for more completions, and for more touchdowns than any Unitas, Sammy Baugh, Bart Starr, or any-

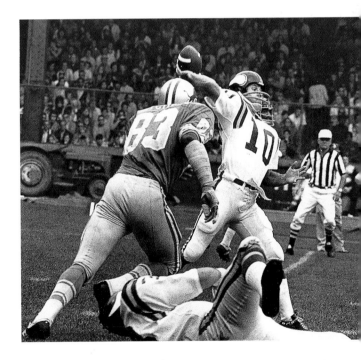

Despite a reputation as a scrambler, Tarkenton set a helmetful of passing records. *(Wide World)*

Tarkenton rolls out to his right in a game for the Giants. *(Wide World)*

one else. During the 1990s, however, his records were eclipsed by Dan Marino.

The son of a Methodist minister, Francis Asbury Tarkenton was named for a missionary of the Revolutionary War period. When he was five, the family moved to Washington, D.C., where Sammy Baugh was filling the air with footballs. Baugh became a hero to Tark.

After the family moved to Athens, Georgia, Francis played quarterback for a YMCA team and in high school. In his senior year at the University of Georgia, he led the Bulldogs to an Orange Bowl win over Missouri.

Once he joined the Vikings, Tarkenton became a scrambler, at least partly out of necessity. The Vikings were an expansion team, new to the league and made up of untried players or those that other teams no longer wanted. The offensive line offered Tarkenton little in the way of protection. Tarkenton scrambled out of terror.

Tarkenton and Minnesota coach Bud Grant teamed up to take the Vikings to three Super Bowls. *(Wide World)*

However, Tarkenton's style didn't appeal to the Vikings coach, Norm Van Brocklin. It seemed like sandlot football to him. The two men had an uneasy relationship. In l966, after Tarkenton asked to be traded, the Vikings dealt him to the Giants.

The New York team, in the midst of a rebuilding program, was not any better than the expansion Vikings. It was a struggle for Tarkenton to get the team to win as many games as it lost.

In 1972, the Giants sent Tarkenton back to Minnesota. But things were different. Van Brocklin was gone; Bud Grant was the coach.

In his 13th NFL season, Tarkenton steered the Vikings into Super Bowl VIII. He had them back the next year for Super Bowl IX and two years later for Super Bowl XI. That's three Super Bowls in four years—and the Vikings lost all three.

Say "Super Bowl" to Fran Tarkenton and he winces. "It's the ultimate humiliation," he says. "People ridicule you and abuse you. They look much more kindly on teams that don't get there than they do on a team that gets there and loses."

When Tarkenton joined the Vikings in 1961, he told the media that he had two goals: "to win an NFL championship and become a millionaire."

Well, he achieved one of those goals, becoming very prosperous in management consulting and the computer software business. Ira Berkow of the *New York Times* visited Tarkenton in Atlanta in 1996. "I've got 14 different projects I'm working on," Tarkenton said.

"Once a scrambler, apparently always a scrambler," Berkow noted.

In a classic scramble, Tarkenton fakes out Cleveland linebacker Jim Houston before setting up to throw. *(Wide World)*

Joe Namath

Born: May 31, 1943
Beaver Falls, Pennsylvania
Height: 6'2"   Weight: 200
High School: Beaver Falls High School
College: University of Alabama
Teams: New York Jets (AFL), 1965–1969;
New York Jets (NFL), 1970–1976;
Los Angeles Rams, 1977
Elected to the Hall of Fame in 1985

The 1960s—the decade of the Vietnam War and the struggle for civil rights, of tie-dyed shirts, flower children, and Janis Joplin records. It was the decade of the counterculture.

In sports, the symbol of the time was a rebel, too, a man named Joe Namath. Tall, good-looking, and slouch-shouldered, Namath signed with the New York Jets in 1965 for something more than $400,000, an extraordinary amount for the day. No football player had ever been paid even half that amount. The contract made Namath an overnight celebrity.

Namath kept adding to the legend. He lived in a penthouse on New York's Upper East Side, tooled around the city in a gray Lincoln convertible, and made no secret of the fact that he liked to party. "Broadway Joe" he was called.

Football? Namath found time for that, too.

Like his role model, Johnny Unitas, Namath was a sharp passer. Nobody set up faster or got rid of the ball quicker. And although people didn't always realize it, Namath was a canny play caller, too.

Namath was the first quarterback in history to exceed 4,000 passing yards in a season. *(Wide World)*

(Below, center) Keeping a wary eye on rushing defenders, Namath hands off to running back Bill Mathis during Super Bowl III. (Wide World)

(Below, bottom) During his playing days, Namath also pursued a career in Hollywood. Here he poses with Ann-Margret, a costar. (Avco Embassy Pictures)

(Above) When it came to setting up and releasing the ball, no one was faster than Namath. (George Sullivan)

When he was on the field, there was no doubt who was in charge out there. "A quarterback doesn't come into his own," Johnny Unitas once said, "until he can tell the coach to go to hell." Namath was in that category.

In high school, Namath starred in baseball and basketball as well as football, but he preferred football. After being recruited by several colleges, he settled on Alabama.

Namath guided the Crimson Tide to three banner seasons. To the legendary Bear Bryant, he was "the greatest athlete I ever coached."

In the 1965 college football draft, Namath was selected by both the NFL's St. Louis Cardinals and the New York Jets of the rival American Football League. Namath picked the Jets—and riches.

Namath was the AFL's Rookie of the Year in 1966. In 1967, Namath steered the Jets to a division title and ended up throwing for 4,007 yards, becoming the first quarterback in history

to exceed 4,000 yards for a season.

In the AFL championship game in 1968, Namath staged one of his finest performances. The Jets trailed the Oakland Raiders, 23–20, in the game's closing minutes. With a first down on the Oakland 6, Namath sent Don Maynard on a slant pattern, and drilled the ball to him just as Maynard crossed the goal line.

It was Namath's third TD pass of the game. The Jets hung on to win their first league title.

Two weeks later, the Jets faced Baltimore in Super Bowl III. At a banquet several days before the game, Namath declared, "I think we'll win it; in fact, I guarantee it."

People snickered. The Jets were 17-point underdogs. Everyone knew that they were going to get clobbered. Namath's prediction made him look like a loudmouth clown.

But once the game got under way, Namath was an artist, running the Jets' attack with confidence and precision. Time after time, he sent fullback Matt Snell smashing into the right side of the line for gains of 5 and 6 yards. And when the Colts blitzed, Namath would pick it up and beat the blitz with quick passes. The Jets won, 16–7.

If Joe Namath never threw another pass, that win assured him lasting fame. There had been two previous contests between NFL and AFL teams, and both had been won convincingly by NFL teams. The Jets' victory was the first by an AFL representative in the series of championship games that would come to be known as the Super Bowl. The win was evidence that the upstart league was at least the equal of the old, entrenched, and often snobby NFL.

Injuries were a big part of Namath's career in

Namath tunes up before a game at Shea Stadium. *(George Sullivan)*

the years after. His bad knees required frequent surgical repair. He broke a wrist and suffered a separated shoulder. Although seldom without pain, his courage and toughness never dimmed. In 1976, Joe was benched, and the next year he signed as a free agent with the Los Angeles Rams. He spent 1977, his last year as a pro, in a backup role.

Namath, during the 1980s and 1990s, was still a presence in New York, enjoying a lucrative career as a TV pitchman. He once confessed that his ambition was to become known as "a good quarterback, not a rich one." He apparently has had it both ways.

Namath spent his final season with the Los Angeles rams. *(Wide World)*

Len Dawson

Born: June 20, 1935   Alliance, Ohio
Height: 6'1"   Weight: 195
High School: Alliance High School
College: Purdue University
Teams: Pittsburgh Steelers, 1957–1959;
Cleveland Browns, 1960–1961; Dallas Texans
(AFL), 1962; Kansas City Chiefs (AFL),
1963–1969; Kansas City Chiefs (NFL),
1970–1975
Elected to the Hall of Fame in 1987

From the time the American Football League began to play a full schedule of games in 1960 until its merger with the NFL almost a decade later, AFL players and coaches yearned for the opportunity to prove the new league was as good as or better than the old, established NFL.

Len Dawson and the Kansas City Chiefs got two chances. The first AFL-NFL showdown—called the World Championship Game but now known as Super Bowl I—came in 1967, the Green Bay Packers vs. Dawson and the Chiefs. The Packers were heavy favorites.

For most of the first half, the teams fought on even terms. Early in the third quarter, when Dawson pedaled back to throw, a pair of Packers blitzed. Instead of holding on to the ball and taking the loss, Dawson fired a wobbly desperation pass that was intercepted by safety Willie Wood, who raced all the way to the Chiefs' 5-yard line. The Packers scored on the next play.

What confidence the Chiefs had oozed out of them after that, and the Packers rolled to a 35–10 win.

Embarrassed by the defeat, Dawson promised,

Dawson holds the AFL's record for touchdown passes, with 182 of them. *(Wide World)*

"We'll be back, no matter how long it takes." It took three years, or until Super Bowl IV.

The Minnesota Vikings were the opposition, and again the Chiefs were underdogs. But Dawson shredded the Viking defenses with his on-the-money passes. The Chiefs led, 16–0, at halftime. This time there was no letdown. A third-quarter Dawson pass boosted the Chiefs into a 23–7 lead, and that's how the game ended. Dawson had controlled the game's tempo, completing 12 of 17 passes and, during one stretch of 18 plays, perplexing the Minnesota defense by calling 18 different formations. His performance that day earned Dawson the game's MVP award.

Len Dawson was a smart quarterback, known for his ability to pick the right play at the right time. Calm and poised no matter the situation, he threw the ball with tremendous accuracy.

Dawson didn't have much of a chance to display his talents during the early stages of his career. Drafted by Pittsburgh in 1957 after winning All-America honors at Purdue, Dawson spent three years as a backup with the team before being traded to Cleveland. Two seasons with the Browns followed. Again, he seldom played.

A turning point came in 1962. Hank Stram, who had been an assistant coach at Purdue when Dawson was the team's quarterback, had become

Under coach Hank Stram at Kansas City, Dawson often passed from what Stram called a "moving pocket." *(Kansas City Chiefs)*

Dawson sets up to pass against Green Bay in the first Super Bowl. *(Wide World)*

head coach of the AFL's Dallas Texans. He remembered Dawson as a sharp passer and cool strategist. Once Lenny engineered his release from Cleveland, Stram grabbed him.

It didn't take Dawson long to become a star. In his first season with the Dallas team, he passed for 29 touchdowns, won Player of the Year honors, and led the Texans to the AFL championship.

The Dallas team switched to Kansas City in 1963 and became the Chiefs. Dawson ended up quarterbacking the club for a total of 14 seasons. The league's leading passer four times, he steered the team to three AFL titles and got them to the Super Bowl twice.

In 1975, at the age of 40, Dawson was still firing footballs for the Chiefs. He finished as the third leading passer in the NFL that season. After 1975, his 19th pro season, Dawson retired to devote himself full-time to his career as a sportscaster.

Super Bowl IV was Dawson's finest hour. Each of the Kansas City players wore a patch on his jersey that said "AFL-10." It referred to the 10-year existence of the AFL, which was merged into the NFL following the game. With the Chiefs' decisive victory over the Vikings, Len Dawson took the AFL out in style.

Johnny Unitas

Born: May 7, 1933   Pittsburgh, Pennsylvania
Height: 6'1"   Weight: 195
High School: St. Justin (Pittsburgh) High
School
College: University of Louisville
Teams: Baltimore Colts, 1956–1972;
San Diego Chargers, 1973
Elected to the Hall of Fame in 1979

In the summer of 1955, not very long after his 22nd birthday, Johnny Unitas faced a crisis. He had just been released by the Pittsburgh Steelers, told he didn't measure up to pro football standards. He had no job and his future was bleak.

Yet Johnny knew he was good. He had been a star at the University of Louisville and the Steelers had picked him in the NFL draft. He felt that Pittsburgh hadn't given him a chance to prove himself.

The skinny, six-foot-one Unitas took a construction job that fall and played quarterback for the Bloomfield Rams, a semipro club.

The next spring, Unitas got a second chance when he was invited to work out for the Baltimore Colts. He began the season as a backup to quarterback George Shaw. When Shaw got injured, Unitas took over.

The Colts, a team that had come into existence in 1953, had never had a winning season. Quickly, Unitas helped to change that. With his sharp pass-

Four times during his career, Unitas led the NFL in passing yardage. *(Wide World)*

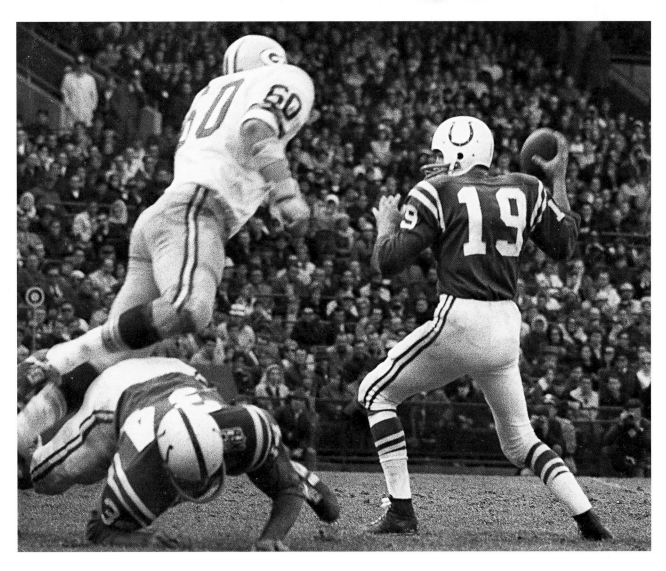

Unitas is unruffled despite the Green Bay blitzer. *(George Sullivan)*

es and gifted play calling, Unitas helped make the Colts contenders in 1957. The following season, Baltimore played the New York Giants for the NFL title.

The game took place on a dark Sunday afternoon at floodlit Yankee Stadium. One of the most dramatic games ever played, it earned a special place in pro football history.

With seven seconds remaining, Steve Myhra of the Colts kicked a field goal, sending the game into "sudden death," an overtime period, the first in NFL history. The Giants won the toss, elected to receive, but couldn't move the ball, and punted.

Soon it was Baltimore's ball on their own 21. Unitas moved the Colts expertly, mixing sweeps and draw plays with short passes to Ray Berry. Once, on a crucial third-down play, he called a hook pass to Berry, but when he saw the New York defensive back lose his footing and fall, he motioned Berry to go deeper. The play got 20 yards and a first down.

A quick trap brought the ball to the Giants' 20. A field goal would win it. But Unitas wasn't through. Another pass to Berry and a short run put the ball on the New York 8.

Then came a daring call. With the Giants look-

Unitas holds an ice pack to a knee he injured in a game against the Bears in 1965. The injury later required surgery. *(Wide World)*

ing for a running play, Unitas fired a sideline pass to Jim Mutscheller. On the next play, Alan Ameche bulled into the end zone for the touchdown, giving the Colts a 23–17 win.

So ended what has come to be called "the greatest football game ever played." And Unitas, who only a few years before was earning $6 a game, was on his way to becoming a football legend.

It wasn't merely his strong and accurate arm that enabled Unitas to win ball games. He had the knack of being able to "look off" defensive backs, seeming to target one receiver, then throwing to another. He was also a master at analyzing opposition defensive setups, and then exploiting them.

When it came to passing, Unitas rewrote the record book, throwing more passes and completing more than any quarterback in history up to that time. During one stretch, Unitas threw touchdown passes in 47 consecutive games, a record that still stands.

Unitas never had much to say. He wasn't emotional. Yet through his enormous skills and confidence, he commanded the respect of his teammates. No one questioned his leadership for a second. Twice, in 1957 and 1967, he was the NFL's MVP.

Unitas's career ended as it began, without any fanfare. He had been dealt to the San Diego Chargers, and one day on the practice field he walked over to the coach and told him he couldn't do the job anymore and had decided to step down. Then he trotted off the field.

In the early 1970s, when pro football was celebrating its first 50 years, Unitas was named the best quarterback of football's first half century. To more than a few observers that's not enough; they say that he is the best of all time.

(Above) Unitas was known as a master at analyzing opposition defensive set-ups. *(George Sullivan)*

(Left) In Super Bowl III against the New York Jets, a grim-faced Unitas, recovering from an arm injury, watches from the sidelines. The Jets won, 16–7. *(George Sullivan)*

Bart Starr

Born: January 9, 1934
Montgomery, Alabama
Height: 6'1"   Weight: 205
High School: Sidney Lanier (Montgomery)
High School
College: University of Alabama
Team: Green Bay Packers, 1956–1971
Elected to the Hall of Fame in 1977

(CBS-TV Sports)

One great play that stands out in Bart Starr's memory is a running play, not a pass. It came in a game for the NFL title that matched the Packers against the Dallas Cowboys.

Played in Green Bay on the last day of the 1967 season, it's come to be called the "Ice Bowl" game. The temperature was 13 degrees below zero at game time. It was so cold that the officials could not blow their whistles because the metal ripped the skin from their lips.

Sixteen seconds were left. The Packers trailed, 17–14. They had the ball on the Dallas 1-yard line.

A field goal would send the game into an overtime period. But the Packers did not want a tie.

At the sideline during a time-out, Starr spoke to Vince Lombardi, the Packers' stocky, bullnecked coach. "I can sneak the ball in," Starr said.

"Then do it," Lombardi answered, "and let's get the hell out of here!"

When the center slapped the ball into his hands, Starr tucked it to his belly, veered to his right behind a pair of ferocious blocks, and smashed his way into the end zone. The final score was 21–17.

The Green Bay Packers were pro football's powerhouse team of the 1960s, capturing one championship after another. But for sheer drama the team's stunning win in the Ice Bowl is unrivaled.

Starr's arm, his ballhandling skill, and his poise and intelligence helped to make him one of the NFL's great field leaders. In the period from 1960 to 1967, Starr's won-lost record was a spectacular 82–24–4.

Pro football had never had a quarterback that could pass with the accuracy of Bart Starr. He

(Left) Besides his brilliance as a passer, Starr was a canny play caller and slick ball handler. (CBS-TV Sports)

(Below) Starr (number 15) bulls his way across the goal line to score the winning touchdown against the Cowboys and to bring the Packers the 1967 NFL championship. (Wide World)

established the NFL record by throwing 294 consecutive passes without an interception. (That record was unsurpassed until the 1990–91 season, when Bernie Kosar of the Cleveland Browns threw 308 passes without getting intercepted.)

Success didn't come easily for Starr. In his final season at the University of Alabama, he was benched by a coach who decided to play mostly sophomores. Then he was ignored in the NFL draft until the 17th round. He went on to endure three frustrating seasons of mostly bench sitting with the Packers, a pitiful team at the time.

Change came when Vince Lombardi took over in 1959. Before long, Green Bay was being called "Title Town, U.S.A."

The bigger the game, the better Starr seemed to perform. Before the Super Bowl came into existence, the two NFL conference winners played for the league championship. Starr quarterbacked the Packers to the NFL title in 1961, 1962, 1965, and 1966.

Bart seemed to thrive on Super Bowl pressure.

The season of 1971 was Starr's last as a player. He became an assistant coach for the team in 1972 and took over as head coach in 1975. Coaching brought him little pleasure. In his nine years as coach, he was never able to get the Packers to win consistently.

Starr's most pleasant memories relate to his days as Green Bay's quarterback. One occurred in 1970, the year before he retired. The people of Green Bay held "Bart Starr Day." There were congratulatory speeches, gifts, and a long and boisterous standing ovation from the hometown fans.

The president of the United States, Richard M. Nixon, was the featured speaker. "The 1960s will be remembered as the decade in which football became America's No. 1 sport," Nixon said.

"The Packers were the No. 1 team and Bart Starr was the No. 1 quarterback."

Indeed, it was true.

In Super Bowl I in 1967, in which the Packers faced the Kansas City Chiefs, Starr picked at and probed the Kansas City defenses until he found the weak spots, then broke open the game with his precision passes.

Super Bowl II, with the Oakland Raiders the opposition, was almost a replay. Again, Starr began cautiously, then crushed the Raiders in the second half. Starr was named the MVP of both Super Bowls I and II.

Bobby Layne

Born: December 19, 1926   Dallas, Texas
Height: 6'1"   Weight: 205
High School: Highland Park (Dallas) High School
College: University of Texas
Teams: Chicago Bears, 1948; New York Bulldogs, 1949; Detroit Lions, 1950–1958; Pittsburgh Steelers, 1958–1962
Elected to the Hall of Fame in 1967

Bobby Layne was no Joe Montana, no Johnny Unitas, no model quarterback. He had a chunky build, wasn't particularly graceful, and his passes had a wobble to them.

But form wasn't important to Bobby Layne. Winning was what counted. It didn't matter whether he threw a perfect spiral. He got the job done.

During a game, Layne would pick and probe, looking for defensive weaknesses. At the critical moment, he'd strike. He had a masterful flair for what was dramatic.

The 1953 NFL championship game, Layne's Detroit Lions versus the Cleveland Browns, is a case in point. With three minutes to play, the Lions trailed, 16–10, and had 80 yards to go for a touchdown. In the huddle, Layne told his teammates, "Y'all block, and ol' Bobby'll pass you right into the championship."

And he did. Layne hit Jim Doran with a pass that netted 17 yards. Then, after two incompletions, he threw to Doran again for 18 yards. After Cloyce Box grabbed one of Layne's tosses for 9 yards, Layne kept the ball and got 3 yards on a dive play.

Leaning on crutches after having suffered a broken ankle, Layne congratulates Detroit quarterback Tobin Rote after Rote led the Lions to the 1957 Western Conference title. It is hard to believe today that Rote was smoking a cigarette after the game! *(Wide World)*

Layne looks anxiously for a pass receiver while being rushed by the Detroit Lions. *(Wide World)*

With it first down on the Cleveland 33, Layne hit Doran with a deep pass and Doran scampered into the end zone. The Lions won, 17–16.

Paul Brown, the legendary coach of the Cleveland Browns, referred to Layne as "the best third-down quarterback in football."

And George Halas, owner-coach of the Chicago Bears, admitted, "If I wanted a quarterback to handle my team in the final two minutes, I'd have to send for Layne."

Layne himself believed that the NFL's top quarterbacks were about equal in terms of talent. "They can all throw with exceptional ability," he said. "Most of them can run adequately enough to keep the defense honest. And most are intelligent play callers.

"The important item is to have the team believe in you." To Layne, that was the "big secret" of quarterbacking success.

Although he worked hard and was always prepared for games, Layne never made any secret of the fact that he liked to have fun. His off-the-field antics occasionally earned him unwanted headlines that cited his inability to drive well after drinking.

Layne learned the ins and outs of being a T formation quarterback in 1947 during his senior year at the University of Texas, where he won All-America honors and attracted the interest of several pro teams. He signed with the Chicago Bears. After a year of sitting on the bench in Chicago, Layne was traded to the New York Bulldogs. A pitiful team that played before mostly empty seats, the Bulldogs were renamed the New York Yanks for the season of 1950, then folded. "You probably don't remember the Bulldogs," Layne said in his book, *Always on Sunday.* "You shouldn't!"

From the Bulldogs, Layne was sold to the Detroit Lions, and there the years of glory began. In 1952, Layne, who led the league in completions, yards gained passing, and touchdown passes, steered the Lions to the NFL championship, downing the Cleveland Browns in the title game. The following year, Layne's pass to Jim Doran brought the Lions another title.

Layne suffered a broken ankle in 1957 and was traded to Pittsburgh during the season that followed. The Steelers hadn't had a winning season in a decade. "It was the New York Bulldogs all over again," said Layne.

Layne managed to get the Pittsburgh team on the winning track for a while, but he was hampered by injuries in his final seasons with the team and the Steelers struggled. After he retired as a player in 1962, Layne settled in Lubbock, Texas, where he became a successful businessman.

Layne, who died in 1986 at the age of 59, was inducted into the Hall of Fame in 1967, the minimum five years after his final season. Of the 54 all-time greats that had been so honored up to that time, only one other had been selected so quickly.

Otto Graham

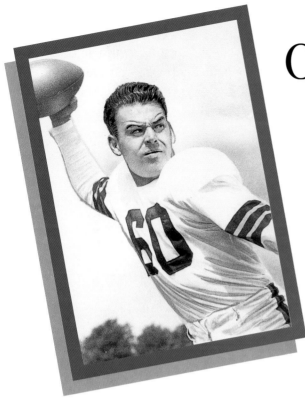

Born: December 6, 1921   Waukegan, Illinois
Height: 6'   Weight: 210
High School: Waukegan High School
College: Northwestern University
Teams: Cleveland Browns (AAFC),
1946–1949; Cleveland Browns (NFL),
1950–1955
Elected to the Hall of Fame in 1965

If you had to select the best quarterback of all time, and your choice was based on the number of division and league championships that he won during his career, then your pick would have to be Otto Graham of the Cleveland Browns. In his 10 years of service, Graham's team never failed to take part in the title game. That's almost like quarterbacking in 10 straight Super Bowls.

The Browns were members of the newly formed All-America Football Conference (AAFC) when Graham joined the team in 1946. He led the Browns to the league championship four years in a row, or until the league folded in 1950.

After the Browns became members of the National Football League, Graham was almost as consistent. He guided the NFL Browns to six consecutive division championships and three league titles.

Graham excelled as a passer. He was known for his long, high-arcing passes that settled light as a feather into the hands of the receiver, and he was remarkably accurate with them.

In college, at Northwestern, Graham won All-America honors, not in football, but basketball. *(Wide World)*

51

After faking a handoff, Graham keeps the ball, skirts right end, and dives into the end zone, as the Browns beat the Rams, 38–14, for the NFL championship. *(Wide World)*

Graham could also throw bullets. His sideline passes to end Mac Speedie were virtually unstoppable. Speedie would break straight downfield, then cut for the sideline, angling back slightly to avoid the defensive back covering. An instant before Speedie stepped out of bounds, Graham would nail him with the ball. Speedie led the AAFC in pass receptions in 1949 with 62, and the NFL in pass receptions in 1952, again with 62.

Like Joe Namath and Johnny Unitas, Graham was fearless in waiting until the last moment to throw the ball. Getting pounded by a defensive lineman never seemed to unnerve him.

And game pressure heightened his skills. Against the Los Angeles Rams in the first meeting of the champions of the AAFC and NFL, Graham was cool, leading a last-ditch drive that salvaged a 30–28 win for the Browns.

Otto Graham was a born athlete, skilled in several sports. At Northwestern, he won All-America honors in basketball and as a running back—a tailback—on the football team, a role he sometimes played with the Browns as well.

One thing Graham didn't do was call the plays

in the huddle. Cleveland coach Paul Brown preferred to send each play in from the bench, a policy that Graham didn't like. But he learned to live with it. "I was working for him; it was my duty to follow orders," Graham once recalled. "I played the game the way he wanted it played."

After the 1954 championship game, in which he threw four touchdown passes, Graham announced that he was retiring, although he was only 33. He had had enough of the discipline that football required. He no longer had any wish to go to training camp and be away from his family for six or seven weeks.

That year, when the Browns started playing their preseason games, Graham's absence was easy to perceive. The team had no spark, no scoring punch, and lost one game after another.

Coach Brown put in a call to Otto. "Forget about retiring," he said. "Come back; we need you!" Reluctantly, Graham agreed.

The team's offense was shaky at the start and the Browns lost the opening game of the season. But they won six in a row before losing again.

In the title game against Los Angeles, Graham was as good as he had ever been. In the third quarter he scored two touchdowns himself and in the final period he passed for another in a 38–14 romp for the Browns.

After the game, Graham announced he was retiring—again. This time he really meant it.

While Graham earned lasting fame for his passing ability, he also carried the ball. Here he scores against the Los Angeles Rams in the 1955 NFL title game, won by the Browns, 38–14. *(Wide World)*

Sammy Baugh

Born: March 17, 1914   Temple, Texas
Height: 6'2"   Weight: 180
High School: Sweetwater (Texas) High School
College: Texas Christian University
Team: Washington Redskins, 1937–1952
Elected to the Hall of Fame in 1963

Baugh first won acclaim for his passing skills at Texas Christian University. *(Wide World)*

When the NFL selected an all-time team as part of its 75th-anniversary fanfare in 1994, Sammy Baugh was the pick as quarterback. And there were no arguments.

Baugh, who retired as a player in 1952, had 16 spectacular seasons as field leader for the Washington Redskins. Many believe that he was the greatest player the game has known.

Certainly no quarterback was as versatile. Baugh won six league passing and four punting titles—yes, *punting!*—with the Redskins. In 1940, he averaged a sensational 51.4 yards per punt, setting an NFL record that still stands.

Besides quarterbacking and punting, Baugh also toiled as a defensive back. And he was an outstanding one. In 1943, he led the NFL in passes intercepted with 11.

Statistics tell only a small part of Baugh's story. His arrival on the pro scene opened a new chapter in pro football. Before Baugh, football offense was based on the ground game, on slants, plunges, and an occasional end run. Teams seldom passed.

Baugh changed that. Standing straight and erect, Baugh fired bullet passes with a quick, wrist-whipping motion. *Zap!* The ball was there.

Baugh showed everyone that despite its risks, the forward pass was the quickest way to move the ball and score touchdowns. By the time he retired, all teams had learned to bank on the pass as much as the running game. Baugh was football's first "impact" player.

A high school star in three sports, Baugh went to Texas Christian University on a baseball scholarship. A third baseman, he earned his nickname, "Slingin' Sam," for his rocket throws to first base. Baugh starred in both baseball and football at TCU.

After he graduated from college, Baugh was offered a contract in both baseball—with the St. Louis Cardinals—and football. Baugh signed both. He was the Deion Sanders of his day.

But a summer in the minor leagues jolted Baugh's hopes for a major-league career. Hitting was his problem. Fed a diet of curveballs and change-ups, Baugh kept striking out and popping up.

With the Redskins, it was much different. Baugh was a sensation from the beginning.

In Baugh's first 10 years with the team, Washington never finished lower than second in their division. The Skins won the Eastern Division

A rifle-armed third baseman, Baugh once considered a baseball career with the St. Louis Cardinals, but he faltered as a hitter. *(Wide World)*

Baugh retired as a player in 1952 after sixteen seasons with the Redskins. *(Wide World)*

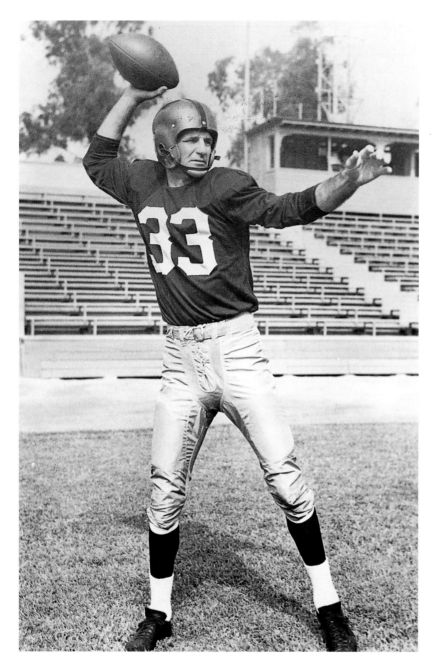

As a passer, Baugh rewrote the NFL's record book.
(Pro Football Hall of Fame)

doctoring sick cattle.

Rodeo was his hobby, and about the only time he left the ranch was to compete. His specialty was calf roping. "He throws a rope the same way he throws a pass," a reporter once said. "He holds the loop close to his head, and when he lets go, the lariat whistles past his ear."

By the time Baugh was ready to retire from football, he had practically rewritten the record book. He held eight all-time records, including most passes completed, most yards gained, most touchdown passes, and highest passing percentage.

He also retired with this tribute from one of his chief rivals, Sid Luckman, quarterback of the Chicago Bears: "Anytime you see a quarterback scramble, or throw on the run, or loft one perfectly in the corner of the end zone for his receiver, that's a reflection of Sammy Baugh. No one ever did those things before him, but a hell of a lot of people sure copied him—including me."

In 1994, *The Sporting News* sent a writer to interview the 80-year-old Baugh on his Texas ranch. Still tall and lean and agile, Baugh said that he played golf five times a week and followed pro football on TV. "On Saturdays and Sundays," he declared, "I watch every damn game I can get."

five times and the NFL championship twice. One sellout crowd after another filled Griffith Stadium to watch him.

After each season, Baugh returned to his wife and three kids and the 7,500-acre ranch he owned in West Texas, about a 90-minute drive north and west of Abilene. There he would get up at dawn and put in a full day fence riding, branding, and

Sid Luckman

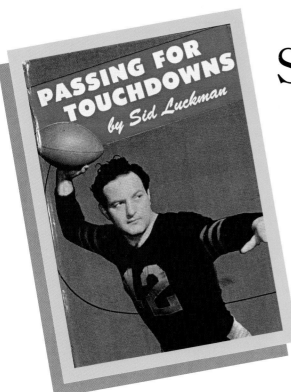

Born: November 21, 1916   Brooklyn, New York
Height: 6'   Weight: 200
High School: Erasmus Hall (Brooklyn) High
School
College: Columbia University
Team: Chicago Bears, 1939–1950
Elected to the Hall of Fame in 1965

Strictly as a passer, Sid Luckman's greatest game came on November 14, 1943. It happened to be Sid Luckman Day. World War II was raging at the time, and Sid was leaving for a tour of duty with the merchant marine. A sellout crowd jammed New York's Polo Grounds to pay tribute to the hometown hero who had starred at Erasmus Hall High School in Brooklyn and New York's Columbia University, and now had returned with the Bears to challenge the New York Giants.

After the speeches and gift giving, Luckman staged a once-in-a-lifetime performance. In leading the Bears to a 56–7 win, he threw seven touchdown passes, setting an NFL record that has endured for well over half a century. While the seven-touchdown mark has been equaled several times, it never has been surpassed.

As pro football's first successful T formation

Luckman (left) and Chicago Bear teammates George McAfee (center) and Ray McLean (right) celebrate after defeating the New York Giants for the 1946 NFL title.
(Wide World)

Luckman not only passed the ball skillfully, he was a runner who was hard to bring down. *(Wide World)*

quarterback, Luckman had more than his share of outstanding games. One other must be mentioned, the 1940 NFL title game, the Bears versus the Washington Redskins.

Luckman was close to flawless that day. His deft handoffs and soft tosses to his backs and men in motion, plus his flawless play calling, bewildered the Redskins. Luckman played only the first half, but when he left the game the Bears led, 28–0. The final score—Bears 73, Redskins 0—looks like a misprint, as *New York Times* sports columnist Arthur Daley noted.

In college, at Columbia, playing out of the single-wing formation, Luckman was a tailback, the running back who lined up farthest from the line of scrimmage. After being voted an All-American in 1938, Luckman was taken in the NFL draft by the Pittsburgh Steelers, then traded immediately to the Bears.

When Luckman joined the Chicago team, he was given two playbooks, which served as his introduction to the T formation. One of the playbooks detailed his assignments for the position of left halfback, the other for quarterback.

Luckman didn't like the T at first. "There you went, darting off the line," he said, "with no more protection than a stray peanut vendor cutting across the field."

But Luckman studied hard, eager to learn what made the T formation work. On road trips with the team, he spent evenings practicing pivots, fakes, and handoffs in his hotel room.

During his rookie season, Luckman was on the bench about half of the time. The next year, 1940, he took over as quarterback for the Bears on a full-time basis.

With Luckman at quarterback, the Bears, the "Monsters of the Midway" as they were called, swept to five Western Division titles and four NFL championships. Sportswriter Dave Eisenberg called Luckman "the coach in the field when he was in the game" and praised him as "probably the smartest quarterback in the history of the game."

The 1950 season was Luckman's last with the Bears as a player. In the years that followed, he kept active in football, helping out as an assistant coach with the Bears and at Columbia.

After Luckman retired, George Halas, who had founded the Bears, owned the team, and coached it until 1976, sought to find a replacement for him. Halas searched in vain. Up until the time he died in 1990, Halas was unable to find a quarterback to equal Sid Luckman in terms of ability and brainpower.

A tailback in the old single-wing formation, Luckman first came to fame at New York's Columbia University. *(Wide World)*

All-Time Records

LEAGUE LEADERS, PASSING

Most Seasons Leading League
6   Sammy Baugh, Washington, 1937, 1940, 1943, 1945, 1947, 1949

Most Consecutive Seasons Leading League
4   Steve Young, San Francisco, 1991–1994

PASS COMPLETIONS

Most Passes Completed, Career
4,134   Dan Marino, Miami, 1983–1996

Most Passes Completed, Season
404   Warren Moon, Houston, 1991

Most Passes Completed, Rookie, Season
274   Rick Mirer, Seattle, 1993

Most Passes Completed, Game
45   Drew Bledsoe, New England vs. Minnesota, Nov. 13, 1994 (OT)

Most Consecutive Passes Completed
22   Joe Montana, San Francisco vs. Cleveland, Nov. 29, 1987 (5); vs. Green Bay, Dec. 6, 1987 (17)

YARDS GAINED, PASSING

Most Yards Gained, Career
51,636   Dan Marino, Miami, 1983–1996

Most Seasons, 3,000 or More Yards Passing
11   Dan Marino, Miami, 1984–1992, 1994, 1995

Most Yards Gained, Season
5,084   Dan Marino, Miami, 1984

Most Yards Gained, Rookie, Season
2,833   Rick Mirer, Seattle, 1993

Most Yards Gained, Game
554   Norm Van Brocklin, Los Angeles vs. N.Y. Yanks, Sept. 28, 1951

Most Games, 400 or More Yards Passing, Career
13   Dan Marino, Miami, 1983–1996

Most Games, 400 or More Yards Passing, Season
4   Dan Marino, Miami, 1984

TOUCHDOWN PASSES

Touchdown Passes, Career
369   Dan Marino, Miami, 1983–1996

342   Fran Tarkenton, Minnesota, 1961–1966, 1972–1978; New York Giants, 1967–1971

290   Johnny Unitas, Baltimore, 1956–1972; San Diego, 1973

281   John Elway, Denver, 1983–1996

273   Joe Montana, San Francisco, 1979–1992; Kansas City, 1993–1994

261   Dave Krieg, Seattle, 1980–1991; Kansas City, 1992–1993; Detroit, 1994; Arizona, 1995–1996

255   Sonny Jurgensen, Philadelphia, 1957–1963; Washington, 1964–1974

254   Warren Moon, Houston, 1984–1993; Minnesota, 1994–1996

254   Dan Fouts, San Diego, 1973–1987

244   John Hadl, San Diego (AFL), 1962–1969; San Diego (NFL), 1970–1972; Los Angeles, 1973–1974; Green Bay, 1974–1975; Houston, 1976–1977

Most Touchdown Passes, Season
48   Dan Marino, Miami, 1984

Most Touchdown Passes, Rookie, Season
22   Charlie Conerly, New York Giants, 1948

Most Touchdown Passes, Game
7   Sid Luckman, Chicago vs. New York Giants, Nov. 14, 1943; Adrian Burk, Philadelphia vs. Washington, Oct. 17, 1954; George Blanda, Houston vs. New York Titans, Nov.19, 1961; Y. A. Tittle, New York Giants vs. Washington, Oct. 28, 1962; Joe Kapp, Minnesota vs. Baltimore, Sept. 28, 1969

INTERCEPTED PASSES

Most Passes Intercepted, Season
42   George Blanda, Houston, 1962

Most Passes Intercepted, Game
6   Jim Hardy, Chicago vs. Philadelphia, Sept. 24, 1950

Most Consecutive Passes, None Intercepted
308   Bernie Kosar, Cleveland, 1990–1991